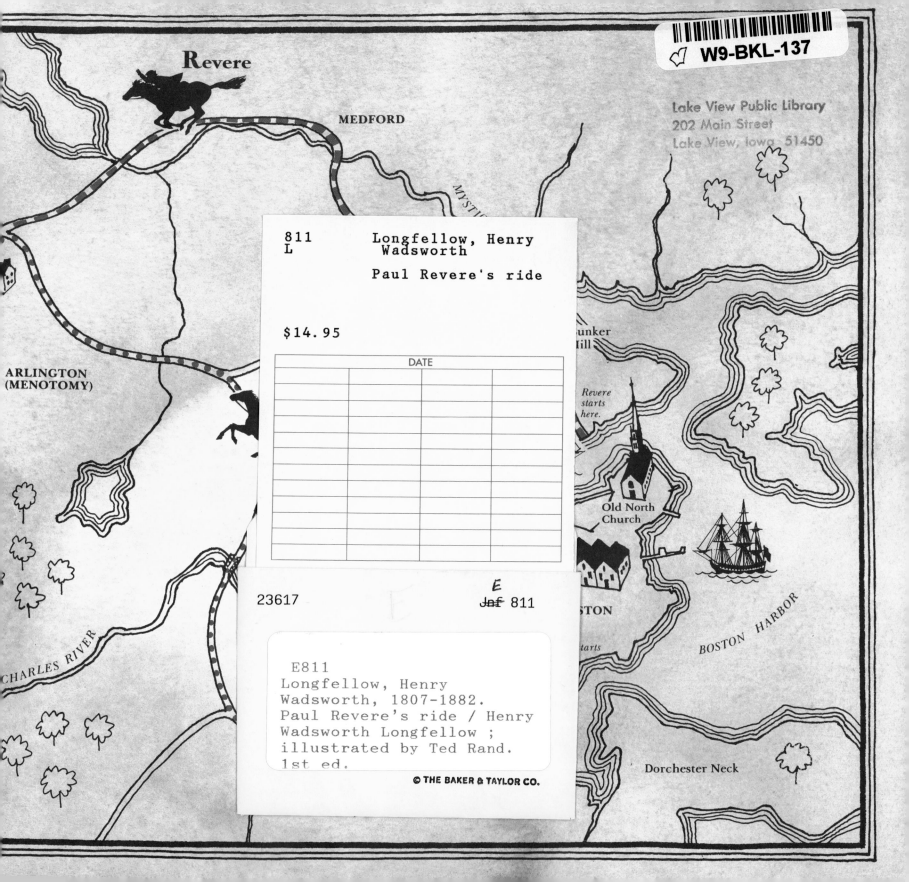

811
L

Longfellow, Henry
Wadsworth

Paul Revere's ride

$14.95

DATE			

PAUL REVERE'S
RIDE

HENRY WADSWORTH LONGFELLOW

PAUL REVERE'S RIDE

illustrated by TED RAND

DUTTON CHILDREN'S BOOKS
NEW YORK

Listen, my children, and you shall hear
Of the midnight ride of Paul Revere,
On the eighteenth of April, in Seventy-five;
Hardly a man is now alive
Who remembers that famous day and year.

He said to his friend, "If the British march
By land or sea from the town tonight,
Hang a lantern aloft in the belfry arch
Of the North Church tower as a signal light—
One, if by land, and two, if by sea;
And I on the opposite shore will be,
Ready to ride and spread the alarm
Through every Middlesex village and farm,
For the country folk to be up and to arm."

Then he said, "Good night!" and with muffled oar
Silently rowed to the Charlestown shore,
Just as the moon rose over the bay,
Where swinging wide at her moorings lay
The *Somerset,* British man-of-war;
A phantom ship, with each mast and spar
Across the moon like a prison bar,
And a huge black hulk, that was magnified
By its own reflection in the tide.

Meanwhile, his friend, through alley and street,
Wanders and watches, with eager ears,
Till in the silence around him he hears
The muster of men at the barrack door,

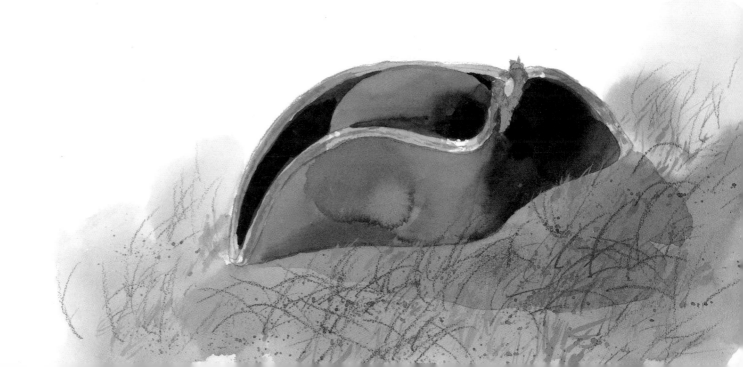

And the measured tread of the grenadiers,
Marching down to their boats on the shore.

Then he climbed to the tower of the Old North Church,
By the wooden stairs, with stealthy tread,
To the belfry-chamber overhead,
And startled the pigeons from their perch
On the somber rafters, that round him made
Masses and moving shapes of shade—
By the trembling ladder, steep and tall,
To the highest window in the wall,

Where he paused to listen and look down
A moment on the roofs of the town,
And the moonlight flowing over all.

Beneath in the churchyard, lay the dead,
In their night-encampment on the hill,
Wrapped in silence so deep and still
That he could hear, like a sentinel's tread,
The watchful night-wind, as it went
Creeping along from tent to tent,
And seeming to whisper, "All is well!"
A moment only he feels the spell
Of the place and the hour, and the secret dread
Of the lonely belfry and the dead;
For suddenly all his thoughts are bent
On a shadowy something far away,
Where the river widens to meet the bay—
A line of black that bends and floats
On the rising tide, like a bridge of boats.

Meanwhile, impatient to mount and ride,
Booted and spurred, with a heavy stride
On the opposite shore walked Paul Revere.
Now he patted his horse's side,
Now gazed at the landscape far and near,
Then, impetuous, stamped the earth,
And turned and tightened his saddle girth;
But mostly he watched with eager search
The belfry tower of the Old North Church,
As it rose above the graves on the hill,
Lonely and spectral and somber and still.

And lo! as he looks, on the belfry's height
A glimmer, and then a gleam of light!
He springs to the saddle, the bridle he turns,
But lingers and gazes, till full on his sight
A second lamp in the belfry burns!

A hurry of hoofs in a village street,
A shape in the moonlight, a bulk in the dark,
And beneath, from the pebbles, in passing, a spark
Struck out by a steed flying fearless and fleet:

That was all! And yet, through the gloom and the light,
The fate of a nation was riding that night;
And the spark struck out by that steed, in his flight,
Kindled the land into flame with its heat.

He has left the village and mounted the steep,
And beneath him, tranquil and broad and deep,
Is the Mystic, meeting the ocean tides;
And under the alders that skirt its edge,
Now soft on the sand, now loud on the ledge,
Is heard the tramp of his steed as he rides.

It was twelve by the village clock,
When he crossed the bridge into Medford town.
He heard the crowing of the cock,
And the barking of the farmer's dog,
And felt the damp of the river fog,
That rises after the sun goes down.
It was one by the village clock,
When he galloped into Lexington.
He saw the gilded weathercock
Swim in the moonlight as he passed,
And the meeting-house windows, blank and bare,
Gaze at him with a spectral glare,
As if they already stood aghast
At the bloody work they would look upon.

It was two by the village clock,
When he came to the bridge in Concord town.
He heard the bleating of the flock,
And the twitter of birds among the trees,
And felt the breath of the morning breeze
Blowing over the meadows brown.

And one was safe and asleep in his bed
Who at the bridge would be first to fall,
Who that day would be lying dead,
Pierced by a British musket-ball.

You know the rest. In the books you have read
How the British Regulars fired and fled—
How the farmers gave them ball for ball,
From behind each fence and farmyard wall,

Chasing the red-coats down the lane,
Then crossing the fields to emerge again
Under the trees at the turn of the road,
And only pausing to fire and load.

So through the night rode Paul Revere;
And so through the night went his cry of alarm
To every Middlesex village and farm—
A cry of defiance and not of fear,
A voice in the darkness, a knock at the door,
And a word that shall echo for evermore!
For, borne on the night-wind of the Past,
Through all our history, to the last,
In the hour of darkness and peril and need,
The people will awaken and listen to hear
The hurrying hoof-beats of that steed,
And the midnight message of Paul Revere.

More About Paul Revere's Ride

At the time of Paul Revere's ride, the thirteen American colonies, which stretched along the eastern seaboard, were ruled by Great Britain. Over many years, the American settlers, who had come mostly from Britain, had grown apart from the faraway mother country. Some people in the colonies felt the Americans should govern themselves. They felt that taxes levied by the British and laws that restricted what the Americans could do were unfair. They didn't like all the British soldiers who had been sent to Boston to keep order and to put down any uprising that might break out.

Paul Revere, a silversmith, was one of the Americans who spoke out and took action against the English king and his government. He and many others felt that war with Britain would surely come.

On the cold, windy night of April 18, 1775, the British soldiers secretly headed out of Boston toward the nearby town of Concord, where, they had heard, the colonists' arms were being stored. The Americans had been expecting such a move. But they hadn't known which route out of Boston the British would choose—whether the British command would decide to ferry the soldiers across the Charles River or march them around its mouth.

Paul Revere's friend, Robert Newman, was picked to watch the army's movements from the tower of the Old North Church. From there, with a good view of the whole city before him, he saw the British begin to move in boats across the water. He signalled to Paul Revere and others, who rode ahead of the soldiers and warned the Americans that the British were coming.

The next morning, the American minutemen, so called because they could be ready to fight in a minute, were up and armed. They fired on the British soldiers, finally forcing them to retreat to Boston. This battle was the first in the American Revolution, which ended with the surrender of the British general Charles Cornwallis to George Washington six years later.

With thanks to Ruth Dunlop and the
Mercer Island Library for their assistance
with research on Paul Revere.
T. R.

Historical note copyright © 1990 by Dutton Children's Books
Illustrations copyright © 1990 by Ted Rand

All rights reserved.

Published in the United States by
Dutton Children's Books,
a division of Penguin Books USA Inc.

Designer: Barbara Powderly

10 9 8 7 6 5 4 3 2

Library of Congress Cataloging-in-Publication Data
Longfellow, Henry Wadsworth, 1807–1882.
   Paul Revere's ride / Henry Wadsworth Longfellow; illustrated by Ted Rand.—1st ed.
      p.   cm.
   Summary: The famous narrative poem recreating Paul Revere's midnight ride
in 1775 to warn the people of the Boston countryside that the British were coming.
   ISBN 0-525-44610-9
   1. Revere, Paul, 1735–1818—Juvenile poetry.   2. Lexington, Battle
of, 1775—Juvenile poetry.   3. Children's poetry, American.
[1. Revere, Paul, 1735–1818.   2. Lexington, Battle of, 1775—Poetry.
3. Narrative poetry.   4. American poetry.]   I. Rand, Ted, ill.   II. Title.
PS2271.P3   1990   89-25630
811'.3—dc20   CIP
                                                                        AC

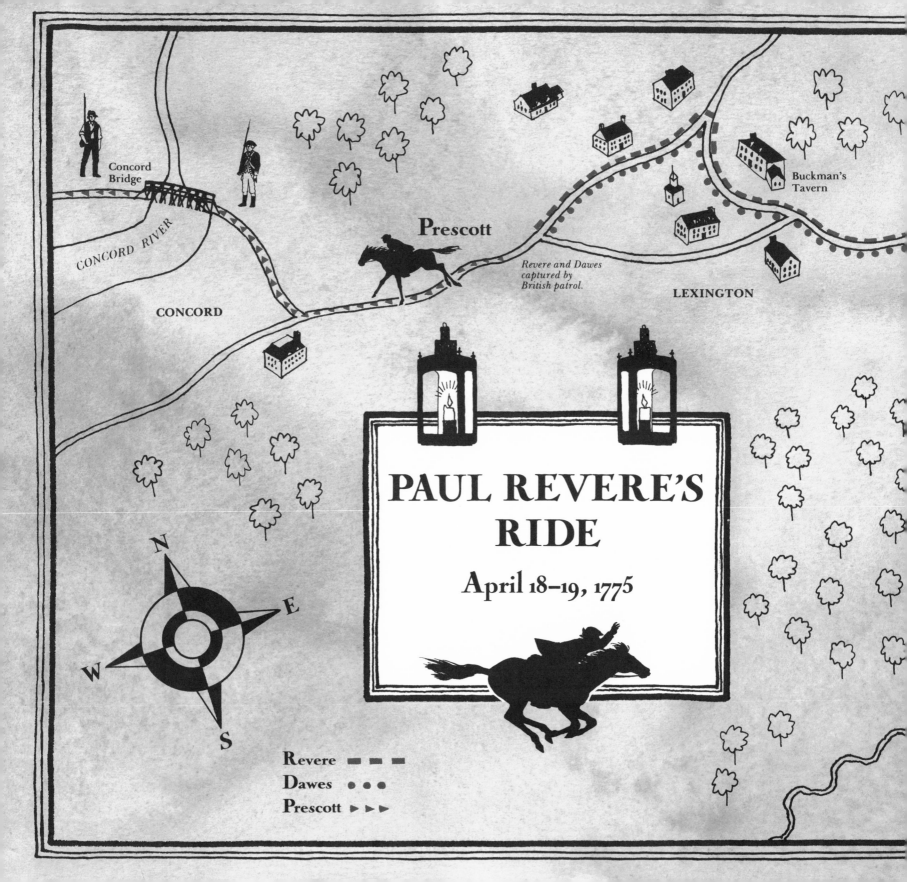

Concord Bridge

CONCORD RIVER

CONCORD

Prescott

Revere and Dawes
captured by
British patrol.

Buckman's
Tavern

LEXINGTON

N

E

W

S

PAUL REVERE'S
RIDE

April 18–19, 1775

Revere ▰ ▰ ▰
Dawes ● ● ●
Prescott ▶ ▶ ▶